Sweetbeet Books
P.O.Box 30921, Chevy Chase, MD 20817

Book and cover design by Peggy Collins, Bookery Design Co.

ISBNs:
978-1-7331539-7-3 (Softcover)
978-1-7331539-8-0 (Hardcover)
978-1-7331539-9-7 (Ebook)

Library of Congress Control Number: 2020919289

Catterfly

Book two

Grows a Garden

By Alma Hammond

Illustrated by Emily Hercock

SWEETBEET BOOKS

To all of us
winged or not,
we all matter
quite a lot!

When last we saw Catterfly,
she zoomed above the midnight sky.

Newly born that day
she had discovered,
she wasn't like other
winged creatures that
hovered.

Catterfly found she not
only had cat-like things.
She also had
antennae and wings!

She met others with wings
that were not exactly like her,
no fangs, whiskers, claws, or fur!

Look at them splash!
she thought,
*Playing in water as a
part-cat is something
I just won't do,
I simply cannot!*

It was on that night, during her very first flight,
rain began to pour and dampen the night.

...terfly's wings, whiskers, and fur got soaked,

...she flew down to land on the branch of an oak.

...e heard a wee voice on the tree from below:

utterfly bidding a tiny, "Hello!"

"Hi," said Catterfly.
"What are you doing
down there?"

m sheltering from the cold, wet night's air!"

"You do know that you could shelter here too.

"lip under the leaf, and do what I do!"

atterfly joined her friend under the leaf.

Hanging by her tail, she at last found relief!

*Hmmm, Catterfly thought,
I can dry off and rest.
This part about me
is truly the best!*

efore long, the sun rose to start a new day,
minding the pair to hurry on their way.

They woke with a thirst that led them to fly
in search of sweet flowers with **nectar** inside.

ey flew by many
wers, so fragrant
d sweet.
JRPRISE!
tterfly landed,
sting with
r feet.

Then, the **butterfly** did something quite funny.
She stuck out her tongue, took a sip, and said, "Yummy!"

"Try this, Catterfly. It's ever so good!"
"You'd like it," she said. "I think that you would!"

Catterfly smiled and stuck her tongue out too.
was straw-like but scratchy, like a cat's tongue. Who knew?

As the friends had their first tastes at last,
they noticed a lizard closing in on them FAST!

"Quick!" said the **butterfly** friend. "Let's hide!"

She found the right flower and jumped on inside.

Catterfly hid inside a flower too.
She did the very best a part-cat could do!

The lizard crept by, shaking his head.
"I can see they were here," he grumpily said.

When the lizard was out-of-sight, the two returned to feed.

The **pollen** they spread helped the flowers make seeds!

What happened much lat[e]
neither of them knew.

hanks to their thirst,
garden grew!

The End.

About the Author

Alma Hammond is the award-winning author of educational children's picture books which promote diversity and self-worth. For other titles published by Alma, including other books in the Catterfly series, go to www.sweetbeetbooks.com. Alma lives with her husband Bob, dog Stazi, and two cats Violet and Daisy, in Bethesda, MD. When Alma is not writing, she enjoys yoga, cooking, and traveling.

About the Illustrator

Illustrator Emily Hercock has used imaginative digital art technics to bring more than 30 published children's books to life. She lives with her husband Michael and crazy cat Dougal in a small village in Norfolk UK. When not working on illustrations, Emily loves to read, watch films, write, and spend time with friends and family.

Stay tuned for another

Catterfly

adventure, coming soon!

Other books in the series:

Book One: Catterfly is Born
Find out how Catterfly was born and
how butterflies come to be!

Do you like this book?
Tell us why with a review on Amazon!

Butterfly Pollination

See Glossary for definitions!

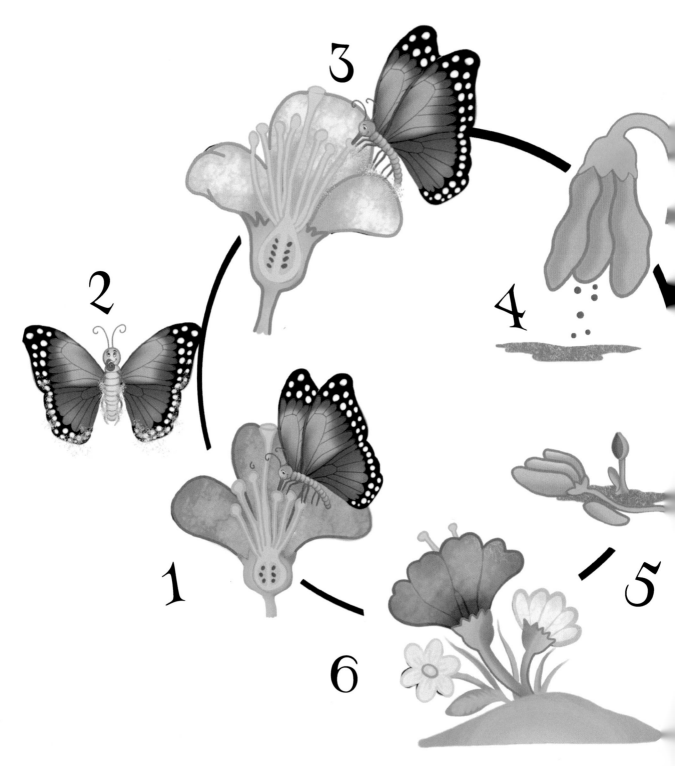

1

A **butterfly** is hungry and takes a drink of the **nectar** deep inside a flower.

2

After enjoying her drink she flies off to find more flowers to drink from, carrying a yellow dust from the first flower, called **pollen** with her.

3

Pollen from the first flower falls off the **butterfly** into the second flower.

4

The **pollen** from the first flower helps the second flower make seeds.

5

When a flower dies, seeds fall to the ground and create more flowers!

6

With more and more seeds falling to the ground, a garden grows.

Fun Facts

1

To escape the rain, **butterflies** fold up their wings and take cover, hanging upside down under leaves or flower petals.

2

Butterflies 'taste' flowers with the tips of their feet before drinking **nectar** or laying eggs.

3

Butterflies have tongues that are like a tube or straw. They're perfect for drinking **nectar** from flowers!

4

Butterflies try to blend in with flowers and shrubs in order to hide from other creatures who might want to eat them, such as spiders, lizards, and birds.

5

Flowers have **pollen** that other flowers need to make the seeds that create more flowers. Some of these even turn into fruits and vegetables! Butterflies take **pollen** from flower to flower when seeking **nectar**, helping gardens grow.

Glossary

antennae: The long, thin body parts on a butterfly's head are called antennae. They help butterflies to feel and smell.

butterfly: A butterfly is an insect with four wings. Butterflies fly mostly during the day, and they help plants to grow by drinking nectar and carrying pollen.

pollen: Pollen is the yellow dust made by flowers. When pollen is carried from plant to plant, it helps to create seeds.

pollination: When pollen is taken from the male part of a plant to the female part, it's called pollination.

nectar: Plants make a sweet syrup called nectar that insects like butterflies love to drink.

Color Me

Made in the USA
Middletown, DE
19 November 2020